WACO-McL

17

W~~~ TX 76701

MISINFORMATION
WHAT IT IS AND HOW TO IDENTIFY IT

DON NARDO

ReferencePoint Press®

San Diego, CA

© 2024 ReferencePoint Press, Inc.
Printed in the United States

For more information, contact:
ReferencePoint Press, Inc.
PO Box 27779
San Diego, CA 92198
www.ReferencePointPress.com

LIBRARY OF CONGRESS CATALOGING-IN-PUBLICATION DATA

Names: Nardo, Don, 1947- author.
Title: Misinformation : what it is and how to identify it / by Don Nardo.
Description: San Diego, CA : ReferencePoint Press, 2024. | Includes
    bibliographical references and index.
Identifiers: LCCN 2023009467 (print) | LCCN 2023009468 (ebook) | ISBN
    9781678205782 (library binding) | ISBN 9781678205799 (ebook)
Subjects: LCSH: Information technology--Moral and ethical aspects--Juvenile
    literature. | Misinformation--Juvenile literature. |
    Disinformation--Juvenile literature. | Deception--Juvenile literature.
Classification: LCC ZA3073 .N37 2024 (print) | LCC ZA3073 (ebook) | DDC
    303.48/33--dc23/eng/20230331
LC record available at https://lccn.loc.gov/2023009467
LC ebook record available at https://lccn.loc.gov/2023009468

CONTENTS

Two Kinds of False Information

During the afternoon and evening of February 21, 2023, Twitter users across the United States were abuzz about a video that had been posted on that popular platform. The post in question showed two dark, rectangular shapes that appeared to be flying through a somewhat fuzzy-looking atmospheric region. The video's caption said that the National Aeronautics and Space Administration (NASA) had taken the video. Moreover, the caption claimed, the two dark objects were alien craft piloted by beings from another world. They *had* to be alien ships, the poster added, because the physical maneuvers they made were clearly beyond the level of current technology.

Disappointment set in fairly swiftly for Twitter followers who had hoped that solid proof of alien visitation had at last been found. In the day that followed, several online sites that regularly fact-check various media claims examined the video and its source. Among them was Snopes, particularly known for its fact-checking accuracy. The Snopes investigators found that the video *had* originated with NASA. However, far from a film showing alien craft, the footage was a digital animation of two NASA satellites, part of the agency's Gravity Recovery and Climate Experiment. The craft had been launched to study ongoing changes in Earth's rivers, oceans, and ice sheets. The digital images had been created to help interested media sources better visualize the program's aims.

Thus, Snopes made clear, the Twitter claim made about alien visitors had been a classic case of misinformation. *Misinformation*, according to Marcel Bruins, editorial director of the online multimedia platform European Seed, refers to false or misleading information that is "not intended to deliberately deceive, manipulate, or inflict harm on a person, social group, organization, or country. Importantly, the spreader does not create or fabricate the initial misinformation content."[1]

Snopes and other fact-checking groups concluded that this was indeed what had happened with the alien visitors story. That rumor had been an example of misinformation in which the individuals who initially spread it did not do so to mislead. In this case, the wrong facts derived from ignorance of the truth, a misunderstanding, or a false assumption.

Disinformation: Purposeful Misinformation

There is also a second kind of misinformation, one in which those who initially spread the rumor intend to mislead people. Such falsehoods are often called *disinformation*. Several examples of this sort of false information appeared during the COVID-19 pandemic that swept the globe between 2020 and 2022. One such rumor, which pervaded numerous media, especially social media platforms such as Facebook and Twitter, was a provocative claim connected to the initial COVID vaccines that appeared early in 2021. According to some social media personalities, these medicines contained metallic substances that caused anyone who received them to become magnetized. Within mere weeks after the first reports of this claim, the internet was flooded with complaints by people across the United States. Some who said they had received the vaccine were certain their bodies had become magnetized, causing coins, spoons, and other metal objects to stick to their skin. A few attempted to show proof that metal or magnets would stick to their skin.

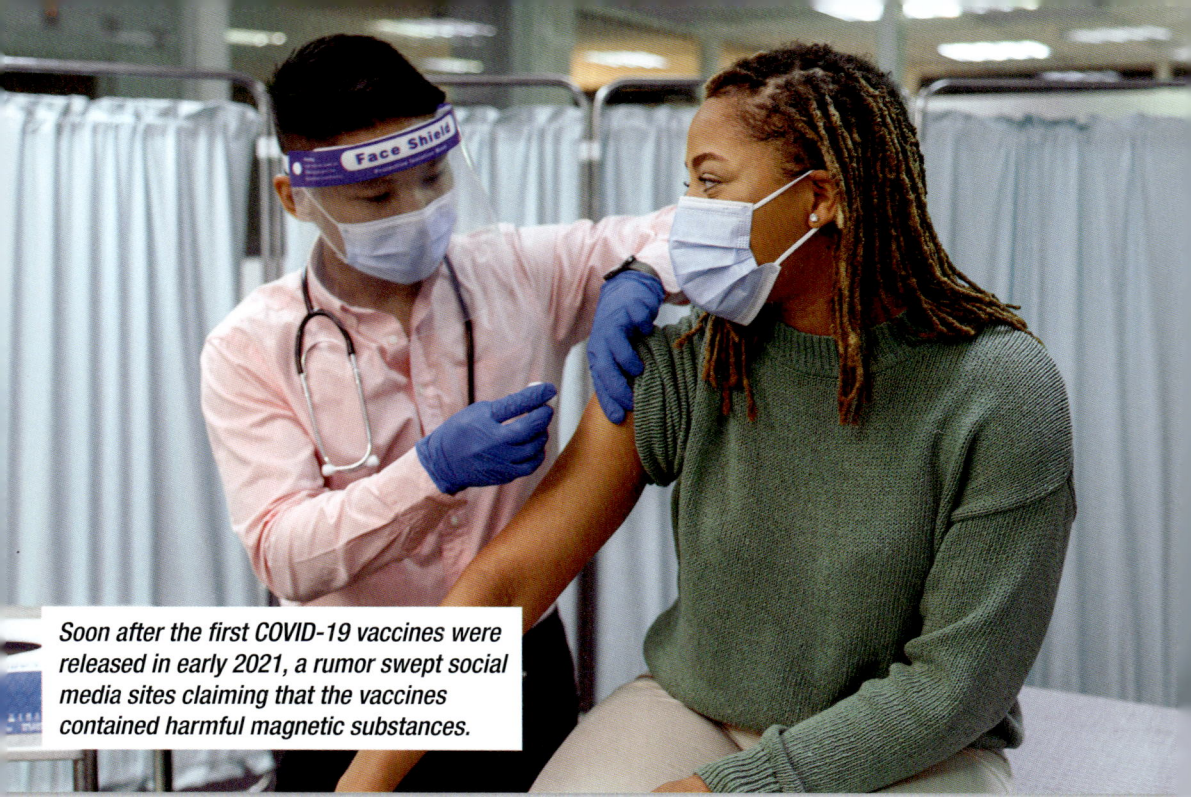

Soon after the first COVID-19 vaccines were released in early 2021, a rumor swept social media sites claiming that the vaccines contained harmful magnetic substances.

It did not take long for scientists and other experts to debunk this magnetic effect. Most simply showed that surface tension and skin oils can make objects stick briefly to skin. The US Centers for Disease Control and Prevention (CDC) stated in a bulletin released in June 2021 that the vaccine could not induce magnetism:

> All COVID-19 vaccines are free from metals such as iron, nickel, cobalt, lithium, and rare earth alloys, as well as any manufactured products such as microelectronics, electrodes, carbon nanotubes, and nanowire semiconductors. In addition, the typical dose for a COVID-19 vaccine is less than a milliliter [0.03 ounces], which is not enough to allow magnets to be attracted to your vaccination site even if the vaccine was filled with a magnetic metal.[2]

The chief culprit behind this ridiculous claim was Sherri Tenpenny. A licensed osteopath in Ohio, Tenpenny addressed a state health committee meeting in June 2021 to fight against vaccine requirements and social distancing mandates. Arguing that the vaccines caused human magnetism was only one of her talking points at the meeting and on social media, where she directed viewers to buy her line of health supplements and COVID education modules. But as Ohio state representative and physician Beth Liston said, as a medical doctor, Tenpenny had to know that the magnetism claim was false. In testimony delivered to the Ohio state legislature in the week following the release of the CDC's bulletin, Liston called Tenpenny "a known conspiracy theorist" who is purposely spreading "absurd, uninformed, and dangerous beliefs."[3]

A Common Thread

Whether false information spreads by accident, misunderstandings, or purposeful lies designed to fool people, examples of the phenomenon share a common thread—namely, they are potentially harmful to either specific individuals or society in general. For example, widely believed false information about COVID-19 and vaccines caused some people to distrust the medical establishment and other sciences. In turn, this had adverse effects on the health of thousands of people who normally rely on the knowledge of doctors and other scientists for accurate information about their health and well-being.

"There are arguably wider societal concerns too," World Economic Forum writer Natalie Marchant points out. "Misinformation also threatens our ability and rights as citizens to make informed choices on issues as important as one's own health. It can also undermine, or further undermine, trust in governments and democratic and/or public institutions at a time when they're particularly vital."[4]

> "Misinformation also threatens our ability and rights as citizens to make informed choices on issues as important as one's own health. It can also undermine, or further undermine, trust in governments and democratic and/or public institutions at a time when they're particularly vital."[4]
>
> —Natalie Marchant, contributor to the World Economic Forum

Moreover, misinformation and disinformation often create other problems, such as causing people to make bad decisions for themselves or their families. Furthermore, these falsehoods may motivate voters to support candidates who peddle lies for political gain. For these and other reasons, it is vital that individual citizens, as well as various businesses and organizations, learn to recognize and combat the ongoing and detrimental spread of false information.

CHAPTER ONE

Causes and Spread of False Information

Early in 2020, as the COVID-19 virus started to spread around the world, a strange and disturbing rumor rapidly spread in the United States. It claimed that the ongoing pandemic was not real. Rather, it was an insidious plot designed to cover up a nefarious plan devised by the founder of Microsoft, wealthy entrepreneur Bill Gates. Supposedly, he intended to use the COVID vaccines—then in development—to implant microchips in people. Those devices supposedly would both track people's every move and allow Gates to collect their personal information.

Although most Americans viewed this claim as extremely far-fetched, a sizable minority believed it. A Yahoo! News survey conducted in May 2020 found that 28 percent of Americans accepted it. Among Republicans, most of whom assumed that Gates was a Democrat (however, he is a lifelong Republican), a whopping 44 percent believed the claim.

Various reporters investigated the rumor. They found that no technology capable of making such advanced microchips is even close to being developed, and there was no proof that any of Gates's companies were working on implanted tracking chips. The reality was that he had advocated that people be vaccinated simply as a public service in hopes of helping them avoid contracting the virus. Thus, the rumor was a piece of false information based on and spread through ignorance of technology and fear of a Democratic conspiracy to trample privacy rights.

The Big Lie

Although the microchip claim can be understood through the lens of us-versus-them politics, sometimes false information is not the result of ignorance, misunderstandings, or fear. Instead, it is purposely spread to fool an audience, often the public, and keep alive an atmosphere of fear and distrust. In 2019, President Donald Trump took credit for coining the term *fake news* to describe news stories that painted his presidency in a bad light. Though the term has existed since the late nineteenth century, Trump used it freely to encourage the public to question legitimate news sources. At the same time, Trump made claims about opponents or his own achievements that these legitimate sources debunked as disinformation.

Perhaps the best-known examples of disinformation pushed by President Trump is what journalists have dubbed "the Big Lie."

Protesters march at a November 7, 2020, rally in Helena, Montana. A woman's sign reads "Stop the Steal" in reference to Joe Biden's alleged "theft" of the 2020 election from then-president Donald Trump.

After losing the 2020 presidential election to Democratic challeng-er Joe Biden, Trump refused to concede and insisted the election had been stolen. He and his supporters claimed that the results were tainted by widespread voter fraud and improper counting of ballots orchestrated by Democrats.

Millions of Trump's fans and followers believed this claim, many out of loyalty to him and support for his strong conservative agen-da. Yet thorough examinations of the voting procedures in all fifty states, along with actual vote recounts in several states, found that no significant fraud had occurred. Corroborating this were more than sixty judges, many of them appointed by Trump him-self, who presided over court cases in which the administration's lawyers kept pushing the claim without any evidence of wrong-doing. Even after several of Trump's former aides and assistants revealed that, back in 2020, he had admitted to losing the elec-tion, many of Trump's supporters continued to maintain that he had been robbed of a second presidential term. The press and media expressed concern over these "election deniers" and their influence on future elections, especially because the deniers had access to popular social media platforms to spread such views.

How Social Media Platforms Spread False Information

The millions of followers who continue to believe Trump's false claims about a stolen election demonstrate how easy it is in mod-ern times to persuade large numbers of people to accept misin-formation and disinformation as truth.

Many experts peg social media as the dominant factor in the spread of half-truths and outright lies. Although social media companies have attempted to remove disinformation from their platforms and have even sanctioned violators who perpetuate it, many users still pass on or even amplify questionable views. Cailin O'Connor and James O. Weatherall, both college professors of logic and philosophy, express their concern for the shortcomings of social media platforms, which can easily spread untruths: "In re-cent years the ways in which the social transmission of knowledge

The Lack of Peer Review in the News Business

Some false information spreads through the various social media platforms, and some disseminates through newspapers, magazines, and television and radio shows. No matter how it spreads, one factor that allows it to spread easily and quickly is the absence of sufficient peer review in the process. In the sciences, peer review is the double and triple checking of the accuracy of a book, article, or scientific claim. When researchers submit an article or book, for instance, one or more of their professional peers examines the material to make sure it is correct. All new scientific discoveries or claims are rigorously peer-reviewed many times before being accepted by the scientific community. In the realm of information and news distribution, however, peer review is rare to nonexistent. This is primarily because of the time-sensitive nature of the material. In the news business, the material often consists of breaking news items. And there is a consensus in that industry that such items should be released to the public immediately. So, there ends up being little or no time to peer-review them for accuracy.

can fail us have come into sharp focus. Misinformation shared on social media websites has fueled an epidemic of false belief . . . and, in some cases, lead to a profound public mistrust of basic societal institutions."[5]

There are several reasons why social media platforms enable the spread of false information. Certainly, it is difficult to police and weed out unreliable or false information. Providers use artificial intelligence programs to look for key words relating to disinformation so that it can be removed; some can even identify robot (or bot) accounts that are designed by bad actors simply to broadcast controversial views. However, those who seek to spread disinformation develop ways around the programs. And because viewers still can find these views on platforms with less monitoring, people are aware of the talking points. In addition, many people tend to believe the talking points that seem to fit neatly with their personal or political opinions, especially those opinions that blame others for perceived social ills. Using Twitter as an example, Chris Meserole, a research director at the public policy group the Brookings Institution, explains how the platform's algorithms even help to present those opinions to a wider audience:

Since we're more likely to react to content that taps into our existing grievances and beliefs, inflammatory tweets will generate quick engagement. . . . If a tweet is retweeted, favorited, or replied to by enough of its first viewers, the [site's algorithm] will show it to more users. At [that] point it will tap into the biases of those users too—prompting even more engagement, and so on. At its worse [sic], this cycle can turn social media into a kind of confirmation bias machine, one perfectly tailored for the spread of misinformation.[6]

The Personal Bias Factor

The confirmation bias phenomenon that Meserole mentions describes people's willingness to accept information that confirms their personal ideas and beliefs. If individuals encounter a piece of information on social media that contradicts their beliefs, they tend to question or disbelieve it. Confirmation bias leads people to trust certain news or social media sources above others because they reinforce a specific personal, scientific, political, religious, nationalistic, or social narrative.

A significant problem with this type of echo chamber is that people are less likely to interrogate and fact-check the information or its source. Furthermore, in cases in which the supposed facts and views involved are incorrect, people may blindly accept them as true. In this way, says Karen Douglas, a professor of social psychology at the University of Kent in England, people can be perpetually fooled by "facts" they do not realize are false. They seek out information online, she explains, from particular sources, and they "disregard other sources that contradict their views. . . . If anything, their

> "Since we're more likely to react to content that taps into our existing grievances and beliefs, inflammatory tweets will generate quick engagement."[6]
>
> —Chris Meserole, a research director at the Brookings Institution

attitudes about these particular alleged [facts] can become even more polarized. So people's [biased] attitudes might become stronger . . . as a result of interacting and sharing and consuming this information on social media and on the internet generally."[7] Thus, as Douglas affirms, people who buy into a specific narrative will often unquestioningly accept and defend elements of that narrative even if they are shown to be incorrect.

An Arena to Promote Conspiracy Theories

One kind of misinformation that has proved to spread especially well on social media is the conspiracy theory. As the name implies, conspiracy theories typically involve some sort of secret plot or scheme orchestrated by a powerful political, military, financial, or technical elite. The group's goals are almost always seen as sinister or immoral, and its members supposedly put

According to one conspiracy theory, US government officials staged the September 11, 2001, terrorist attacks so they could curtail Americans' personal freedoms.

their own personal interests above the needs and desires of the public. And in most conspiracy theories, members of the public are portrayed as ignorant, powerless dupes at the mercy of these shadowy forces.

A still-prevalent conspiracy theory insists that the September 11, 2001, terrorist attacks on New York and Washington, DC, were staged by officials at high levels in the US government to curtail personal freedoms and solidify authoritarian control of the masses. This argument remains because the impact of the attacks—increased security at airports, for example—are still visible, and people see these vestiges as examples of a government attempt to rob people of their liberties. And those who believe they have less control over their lives are apt to believe they are the targets of malicious government officials rather than intangible political or social forces that they might not understand or want to accept.

According to psychologists and other experts, it is common for people to suspect the motives of others, especially members of large groups that wield much power in society. Karen Douglas explains, "As far back as we can remember, people have been having these . . . suspicions about the actions of hostile collectives of individuals." This is a scenario in which conspiracies are born and nurtured. Those who are drawn to conspiracy theories, says Douglas, often lack "the tools to allow them to differentiate between good sources and bad sources or credible sources and non-credible sources. So they're looking for that knowledge and certainty, but not necessarily looking in the right places.[8]

> "People are drawn to conspiracy theories when they feel uncertain either in specific situations or more generally. . . . They're looking for that knowledge and certainty, but not necessarily looking in the right places."[8]
>
> —Karen Douglas, social psychologist

Misleading Information in Broadcast News

Although social media platforms are often blamed for providing a forum to spread false information, they are not alone in airing misinformation and disinformation. Mainstream television and radio news organizations sometimes spread incorrect information, at times by mistake and other times on purpose. Nicholas A. Ashford, a professor of technology at the Massachusetts Institute of Technology (MIT), writes that "television and radio are often full of misleading information, both on news programs and in advertisements, and the broadcast gives the information a whiff of legitimacy."[9]

Often the false information, now frequently labeled *fake news*, put out by broadcast media is largely based on political partisanship. Some news organizations lean toward the left, or progressive, end of the political spectrum, whereas others lean toward the right, or conservative, end. The sources on both ends do present a certain amount of factual news, but they also at times slant the content in their preferred direction. They accomplish the latter by either failing to report certain key facts in a news story or by only interviewing guests on air whose personal opinions reflect the bias of the news outlet.

Thankfully, veteran news agencies insist on substantiating facts they report and often retract or correct claims they make in error. Some less reputable broadcasters, though, are more interested in the hype generated by controversy rather than accuracy. For example, noted conspiracy theorist Alex Jones, host of the radio show *Infowars*, continually lied on air, insisting that the 2012 shootings at Sandy Hook Elementary School in Connecticut constituted a hoax. According to Jones, the twenty children and six teachers killed in that incident were actors employed by the administration of President Barack Obama as part of a plan to take guns away from Americans. Jones finally faced justice for his lies, however. In October 2022, after Jones was sued by the victims' families, the judge ordered him to pay tens of millions of dollars in damages. By then, though, his rants had already been absorbed by his roughly 6 million weekly listeners, some of whom were eager to believe that the Obama administration was set to overturn the Second Amendment.

Radio talk show personality and noted conspiracy theorist Alex Jones addresses demonstrators protesting COVID-19 stay-at-home orders at a rally in Austin, Texas, on April 18, 2020.

Causes of Bias in Broadcast News

One reason why broadcast news groups can perpetuate misinformation is because they are under no obligation to present either all the facts or opposing opinions in a news story. However, that was not always the case. "Decades ago," Ashford points out,

> long before there was a technology industry to regulate, the Federal Communications Commission instituted the Fairness Doctrine, a policy that required broadcasters to present diverse points of view on controversial topics. The law, which was designed to ensure that all sides of an issue were presented, was dismantled in 1987 under President Ronald Reagan.[10]

In the absence of the fairness doctrine, a few broadcast news organizations felt free to present a more opinionated or highly biased version of the news. Many outlets still tried to present

Falsehoods from Left-Leaning Occupy Democrats

Occupy Democrats is a left-leaning political organization and advocacy journalism group whose website and Facebook page were created to counter the influence of right-wing media and messaging. According to respected fact-checking websites FactCheck.org and Politifact, Occupy Democrats has posted many false statements on social media.

- On February 27, 2023, a meme posted by Occupy Democrats on Facebook and Instagram claimed that "156 congressional Republicans . . . just voted to RAISE the retirement age to 70." No such vote took place, according to FactCheck.org, a project of the Annenberg Public Policy Center.
- On April 8, 2022, Occupy Democrats posted a statement on Twitter claiming that "the chairman of Virginia's Republican Party made a 'shockingly racist post' about Defense Secretary Lloyd Austin." The Poynter Institute's Politifact rated this statement as false. It says, "[The] racist Facebook post is real, but it was not made by the chairman of Virginia's Republican Party."
- On July 22, 2019, Occupy Democrats posted this statement on Facebook: "Fox 'News' just announced that they will not air Mueller's testimony about his report." This post refers to Special Counsel Robert Mueller's testimony before Congress in connection with his investigation of Russian attempts to disrupt the 2016 election. Politifact rated the posted statement false. Like other media, Fox News provided live coverage of Mueller's testimony.

Quoted in D'Angelo Gore, "Liberal Group's Meme Mentions Nonexistent GOP Vote to Raise Social Security's Retirement Age," FactCheck.org, March 6, 2023. www.factcheck.org.

"Latest False Fact-Checks on Occupy Democrats," Politifact. www.politifact.com.

---

multiple sides of issues, but the damage had been done. Opinion-based news reporting became mixed with factual appraisals of events, leaving many Americans feeling as though no agency could be trusted. Ian Klein, a law student writing in the *Hastings Communications and Entertainment Law Journal*, believes that now "the United States is faced with a crisis of distrust in the media the likes of which it has never seen before. Abject media bias and online fake news have created a situation in which most Americans cannot even name an unbiased news source."[11]

Going hand in hand with opinion-based information dissemi-nated by broadcast news is the fact that critical-thinking skills—especially in relation to media consumption—are not always taught or promoted in educational institutions. Experts point out that many people lack the skills or desire to examine a claim or argument and then evaluate the evidence that the claim or ar-gument presents. They then are unable to separate what is factual from what is either simply opinion or some form of disinfor-mation. The unfortunate result is that large numbers of everyday citizens are partly re-sponsible for being misled by fake news. In Klein's words, 'The burden to think critical-ly, question suspect claims, get information from reputable sources, and hold media outlets accountable for the accuracy and objectiv-ity of their reporting lies upon us as consumers of media."[12] Ac-tive listening and interrogating sources are extremely important at a time when social media and the explosion of information outlets may make it seem like all arguments are valid.

> "The United States is faced with a crisis of distrust in the media the likes of which it has never seen before."[11]
>
> —Ian Klein, a law student writing in the *Hastings Communications and Entertainment Law Journal*

Enabling the Spread of Falsehoods

Whether false information spreads via social media, broadcast sources, or some other means, that process is made easier by certain flaws in both the news distribution system and society itself. Many Americans at times lack the specific knowledge needed to tell whether what they hear or read is right or wrong. And the more that individuals encounter a viewpoint—often in the headline of an article they do not read or the tagline of a social media post—the more they tend to believe in its accuracy. Al-though this phenomenon can influence people's understanding of basic facts, psychology professor Lisa Fazio says it is particularly troubling because "repetition also affects belief in false political headlines and politicians' falsehoods."[13]

Another reason why false information tends to spread quick-ly is because there are few or no consequences for those who disseminate it. Alex Jones's loss in court and order to pay millions of dollars for his lies is a rare exception. In the political arena, there are fears that lying or spouting misinformation is becoming more commonplace. For instance, in recent years both President Biden and former president Trump have been fact-checked by the Associated Press and other organizations, and many of their statements have been found to be inaccurate. Yet there seem to be few repercussions for high-office holders who make erroneous claims. Occasionally, politicians walk back statements to try to manage any fallout; at other times, they insist they have been misinterpreted by a biased media. "It's a tragic indictment of the political process these days," says Mark Sanford, a former Republican governor who lied to the public about an extramarital affair and was censured by his state government. He was disturbed that several other Republican leaders had been caught openly lying between 2016 and 2022 but were not punished for it, as he was. "Truth doesn't matter, words don't matter," he remarks. "You cross lines now, and there are no longer consequences."[14]

Understanding how false information is perpetuated and the toll it takes in a democracy is essential, say O'Connor and Weatherall. They maintain it is

> invaluable to us in our attempts to reach the truth. It is only through a proper understanding of these social effects that one can fully understand how false beliefs with significant, real-world consequences persist. . . . And during an era when fake news can dominate real news and influence elections and policy, this sort of understanding is a necessary step [in combating it].[15]

CHAPTER TWO

How False Information Is Damaging to Society

On Sunday, December 4, 2016, thirty-two-year-old Edgar M. Welch of North Carolina made the six-hour drive to Washington, DC. After parking near Comet Ping Pong, a local pizza shop, he removed a military-style rifle from his trunk and entered the restaurant. Soon after, the patrons of the shop fled. Welch then walked to one side of the shop and began firing at a locked door. Fortunately, no one was killed or injured during the attack.

Not surprisingly, the pizzeria's manager called the police, who speedily arrived and placed Welch under arrest. When they asked him why he had fired at that door, he replied that he had intended to descend to the cellar and save a group of imprisoned children. When the manager and a police officer showed him that the door led to a closet and explained that the building had no cellar, the gunman appeared extremely surprised. Welch said that he had read several articles on the internet that claimed that recently defeated presidential candidate Hilary Clinton and some of her aides were running a pedophile sex ring in the shop's basement. There, supposedly, unknown numbers of children were being horribly abused and possibly killed. Eventually, Welch felt that it was his civic duty to rescue the children.

The shop's operators confirmed to the police that twisted rumors about a torture chamber at the shop had been circulating through social media for over a month. And the

Edgar M. Welch surrenders to police in Washington, DC, on December 4, 2016, after opening fire inside a local pizza shop called Comet Ping Pong.

pizzeria's owners had received numerous death threats from right-wing activists who were naive enough to believe that such a ludicrous claim was true. Welch later admitted that he had not considered that he might be acting on disinformation in the form of lies spread to discredit Clinton. Nor had he recognized that the claim about the sex-trafficking ring made no sense. For instance, it had not occurred to him that, as a former First Lady, Clinton is guarded around the clock by a team of Secret Service agents. These law enforcement officers would never allow her to commit a crime, even if she wanted to. For his gross gullibility and lack of common sense, Welch was later sentenced to four years in prison.

Increasing Distrust of Government

Dubbed PizzaGate by the broadcast media, the incident in Washington, DC, was a clear and scary example of how dangerous and hurtful false information can be. This is especially true when such disinformation spreads through social media and the internet and sways the beliefs of average citizens. As *New York Times* journalists Cecilia Kang and Sheera Frenkel put it, "The baseless notion that Hillary Clinton and Democratic elites were running a child sex-trafficking ring out of a Washington pizzeria spread across the internet. [PizzaGate illustrated] how a crackpot idea with no truth to it could blossom on social media, and how dangerous it could be."[16]

The fact that Clinton was a former US First Lady, as well as a former presidential candidate at the time, closely tied her to the national government. And the PizzaGate incident was one of many instances in which disinformation was designed to sow distrust in government figures. Regrettably, say National Public Radio (NPR) reporters Sarah McCammon and Liz Baker, "widespread acceptance of disinformation is shaping the political process at all levels of government." They continue,

> Conspiracy theories, disinformation, and distrust in the election system have sown controversy, and even violence, at all levels of government in recent months. . . . [In 2020], the FBI foiled a plot to kidnap Michigan Gov. Gretchen Whitmer. Several of the right-wing extremists arrested in connection with the plot appeared to have been influenced by unfounded conspiracy theories.[17]

This distrust of the government is more widespread than many people realize. A 2019 poll by the Pew Research Center found that many Americans do not have much confidence in the federal government in general, no matter which party is in power. For instance, the survey found that only 24 percent of Americans think the federal government should receive more

"[PizzaGate illustrated] how a crackpot idea with no truth to it could blossom on social media, and how dangerous it could be."[16]

—Cecilia Kang and Sheera Frenkel, *New York Times* journalists public confidence than it gets. In comparison, 75 percent of those polled feel it does not deserve any more trust than it presently gets. The Pew survey also found that Democrats and Republicans tend to blame each other for this situation and therefore increasingly distrust members of the other party. In addition, many of those surveyed agreed that this lack of confidence in government is making it harder for politicians to get together and solve the country's many problems. It is also leading citizens like Welch to turn that distrust into open aggression against politicians who are the targets of conspiracy theories and disinformation.

Is American Democracy in Crisis?

Furthermore, tied to the growing distrust of government caused by fake news and conspiracy theories is a growing threat to American democracy itself. A 2022 survey conducted by NPR established that 64 percent of Americans worry that US democracy is in a state of crisis and may possibly end up failing soon. In fact, 70 percent of those polled stated their perception that democracy was more at risk of failing in 2022 than it was in 2021. In a related vein, a 2022 Quinnipiac University study found that 76 percent of Americans see instability in the nation's political system as a larger threat to the country than foreign adversaries.

This increasing lack of confidence in the American democratic system has been driven by a veritable explosion of false information. According to Gabriel R. Sanchez and his fellow scholars at the Brookings Institution, a hefty portion of those untruths consist of purposeful disinformation "deliberately aimed at disrupting the democratic process." As they explain,

> This confuses and overwhelms voters. Throughout the 2020 election cycle, Russia's cyber efforts and online actors were able to influence public perceptions [in the United States] and sought to amplify mistrust in the electoral process by denigrating mail-in voting, highlighting alleged

irregularities, and accusing the Democratic Party of engaging in voter fraud. The "Big Lie" reinforced by President Trump about the 2020 election results amplified the Russian efforts and has lasting implications on voters' trust in election outcomes.[18]

What is more, ongoing claims of election fraud further damaged the country's democratic system by helping to spur the direct attack on the US Capitol building on January 6, 2021. First, Trump convinced millions of his followers that he had won the election; next, he claimed that the vice president's and Congress's certification of the election in the Capitol building could be exploited to reverse the election results. Then thousands of Trump's most ardent supporters showed up in the nation's

Spurred on by claims of election fraud, Trump supporters descend on the US Capitol in Washington, DC, on January 6, 2021.

capital on January 6. Unbeknownst to the public or press at that time, some had already plotted to use the president's bogus claims as justification for storming the Capitol and seizing control of it for him. The degree to which this deception and desecration damaged American democracy can be seen in the widespread disgust expressed by many citizens. According to a Pew study conducted later in 2021,

> A woman in her 60s said [she was] "shocked, horrified, and sad for our country. . . . How could fellow citizens violently enter federal buildings intending to destroy property and possibly harm our leaders?" [Many others] also expressed surprise, incredulity or embarrassment that such an event could happen in the United States. One man in his 60s said, "A slap in the face to democracy, something you would expect to see in a third world nation."[19]

The Growing Threat of Deepfakes

Unfortunately for people in all corners of society, false information, especially when purposefully spread, is in the process of becoming even more believable thanks to the rapid march of advanced technology. It consists of a new kind of computer program commonly called a *deepfake*, which is rapidly spreading. According to Rob Toews, an expert on economic and social trends, deepfake technology "enables anyone with a computer and an internet connection to create realistic-looking photos and videos of people saying and doing things that they did not actually say or do." Several deepfake videos have already gone viral. In one, President Obama uses a swear word to describe President Trump; in another, Mark Zuckerberg admits that Facebook's actual goal is to manipulate its customers. "It does not require much imagination to grasp the harm that could be done if entire populations can be shown fabricated videos that they believe are real," says Toews. "Imagine deepfake footage of a politician engaging in bribery or sexual assault right before an election; or of U.S. soldiers committing atrocities against civilians overseas. . . . In a world where even some uncertainty exists as to whether such clips are authentic, the consequences could be catastrophic."

Rob Toews, "Deepfakes Are Going to Wreak Havoc on Society. We Are Not Prepared," *Forbes*, May 25, 2020. www.forbes.com.

Becoming Isolated from Reliable Information

In addition to breeding distrust in government and threatening the democratic system, false information has done a great deal of damage to the news media. Based on extensive surveys taken of Americans of all walks of life, Pew researcher Lee Rainie concludes that public trust of the news media is steadily declining. "Our work," he says, "shows that people are less trustful of major institutions, including the news media, than they used to be." Rainie points out that although people have numerous news sources that they rely on,

> they don't think that the institution of the news media and the industry of news organizations as a whole is trustworthy. So people tend to go to sources of information that map with their point of view. And we see in our data that Americans don't trust each other the way they used to. They don't think Americans share the same facts that they used to. And so, the charge to people who are in the thick of this new environment is to figure out how to help people find their way to the truth and not make it a hard job. And Americans couldn't be clearer about that. They want to know what's going on, and they want help doing it, and they are looking to journalists to help solve these problems.[20]

As a result of this general mistrust of many media sources, Rainie and other experts say, the public invariably becomes increasingly less well informed about a wide range of issues. One reason this happens, says David A. Graham, a staff writer for *The Atlantic*, is that the more that people distrust news sources in general, the more likely they will be to stop watching or reading some of them. In turn, those individuals will often choose only those news outlets that seem to have a point of

"People are less trustful of major institutions, including the news media, than they used to be."[20]

—Lee Rainie, researcher with the Pew Research Center

view they already agree with. In so doing, people become isolated from information, often of an important nature, that is disseminated by the outlets that were dropped.

Graham notes that, based on studies by Pew and other polling organizations, in recent years this process of information isolation has hurt people who are conservative and tend to vote Republican more than it has people who are progressive and vote Democratic. He explains,

> If people stop reading a website because it's peddling conspiracy theories, that's good news. If they stop consuming any coverage from mainstream outlets like CNN or *The Washington Post* because they believe a story is biased, or because the president has labeled it fake news, that's less positive. While nearly six in 10 Democrats have dropped an outlet over perceived fake news, a full 70 percent of Republicans have. A much larger portion of Republicans has also reduced their overall consumption of news. The *less* politically aware are also 20 percent more likely to have reduced their overall consumption of news than the *more* politically aware. [This means] that people who were already acquiring the least information are now acquiring even less.[21]

Damaging Political Adversaries' Reputations

Another negative outcome of false information is the spread of disinformation about various social groups. This approach is usually employed by one or more political or social factions to spread distrust and provoke denunciation of a particular group. A clear example from the early 2020s was the attempt to smear the name and image of the group Black Lives Matter. Frequently referred to by its abbreviation, BLM, its influence burgeoned in the summer of 2020 after George Floyd, a Black man in Minneapolis,

Minnesota, was murdered by a police officer during a routine arrest. The incident ignited outrage across the country. And groups composed of people of all races joined with Black Lives Matter and staged protests in many cities.

Although most of these demonstrations were peaceful, for political reasons various right-wing conservative groups sought to demonize and discredit BLM. Social media and conservative broadcasts repeatedly made negative references to the group, falsely claiming it routinely fomented riots and other sorts of violence to get its way.

In the weeks that followed, online fact-checking sites easily debunked these claims, but the damage had mostly been done. According to the nonpartisan Center for Information Technology and Society,

The fake news surrounding BLM negatively impacted the organization itself and even increased prejudice and racism towards African Americans: A 2022 study examined the effect of the portrayals of the BLM movement in fake

29

news on people's attitudes toward African Americans. People exposed to fake news about BLM reported more negative attitudes toward Black people than those exposed to accurate news sources. This study highlights the impact that fake news can have on peoples' perceptions of Black people in America.[22]

Violence, Sickness, and Death

Perhaps the worst and most damaging of all the results of false information occur when it causes overt violence as well as sickness and even death. In recent years, many violent episodes based on fake news involved attacks on members of America's Asian American and Pacific Islander communities. In the words of Jonathan Corpus Ong, a professor of global digital media at the University of Massachusetts, Amherst, such assaults were especially numerous "in the wake of the COVID-19 pandemic. When former president Donald Trump blamed China for the coronavirus, his use of racially charged language, such as referring to COVID-19 as the 'Kung Flu' or 'Chinese virus,' corresponded with increased reports of hate crimes against individuals of Asian descent."[23]

Similar outbreaks of violence have been perpetrated by individuals who were duped into believing in QAnon, an absurd conspiracy theory that gained traction online in 2017 and was echoed immediately by right-wing radio talk shows. QAnon was so named because an anonymous social media poster known only as "Q," who claimed to be a high-ranking member of the military and political community, began commenting that the American left was led by a political, business, and celebrity elite who were Satan-worshipping cannibals. This conjecture spread rapidly on 4chan and other right-wing social media and ultimately influenced the actions of people like Edgar Welch. But Welch was not the only convert; a number of those who attacked the US Capitol on January 6, 2021, were QAnon believers. And later that

Public Perceptions of Social Media

The fact that Facebook, Twitter, and most other social media platforms are routinely employed to fool and manipulate the public is not lost on most Americans. Indeed, a large proportion of the US population thinks that such online sources have negative effects on society. According to a July 2020 study conducted by the Pew Research Center, 64 percent, or roughly two-thirds, of Americans feel that social media have various unhealthy effects on the country. In the words of former Pew analyst Brooke Auxier,

> Those who have a negative view of the impact of social media mention, in particular, misinformation and the hate and harassment they see on social media. They also have concerns about users believing everything they see or read, or not being sure about what to believe. Additionally they bemoan social media's role in fomenting partisanship and polarization. . . . Roughly half of Democrats and independents who lean toward the Democratic Party (53 percent) say social media have a largely negative effect on the way things are going in the country today, compared with 78 percent of Republicans . . . who say the same.

Having a healthy distrust of platforms that often spread distrust might aid the fight against misinformation.

Brooke Auxier, "64% of Americans Say Social Media Have a Mostly Negative Effect on the Way Things Are Going in the U.S. Today," Pew Research Center, October 15, 2020. www .pewresearch.org.

year, a California man was arrested for murdering his own children. He told police that he did it because he was convinced that they possessed reptilian DNA, another fantastical element of the QAnon conspiracy theory that claims reptilian beings from an alternate dimension are trying to take over Earth by creating a race of half-human, half-lizard shape-shifters.

QAnon disinformation also influenced the anti-vaccination rhetoric during the COVID-19 pandemic in 2020 and 2021. Some Q supporters claimed the vaccines designed to fight the virus were, in fact, created to brainwash and enslave people to the liberal global elite. Despite the ridiculous nature of the claim, the anti-vax movement peddled such bunk, instilling fear in Americans and others across the globe and causing many people to go unvaccinated. And of those, some ended up contracting the virus and dying. A few of the other false claims about COVID included that it was a biological weapon made in China, that it could be cured by taking certain vitamins, that Black people could not contract it, and that people could catch the virus from a family pet. In this climate of fear, some people simply distrusted science as another form of government mandate designed to steal personal liberties.

Whether it threatens democracy, spreads lies about a political opponent, or causes unnecessary violence or death, false information can damage society in numerous ways. Sebastiaan van der Lans, director of the Trusted Web Foundation, which works toward the goal of posting only truthful information online, asserts, "Fake news creates a false reality that not just one or two people buy into, but thousands, and it creates a reality that those creating the fake news can manipulate to whatever they want it to be. Those lies, if continued to be perpetrated, can turn deadly or threaten societal stability . . . [and can negatively affect] the well-being of an entire nation."[24] But moving beyond national borders, disinformation can sow distrust among countries, prompting people worldwide to question the power of voting, the value of diversity, the benefits of health care, and institutions that have become the backbone of modern civilization.

CHAPTER THREE

Distinguishing Facts from Misinformation

People hope and even expect that news information is true and accurate. In an information age that now entertains so many sources of news and purported facts, it can be difficult for consumers to be sure they are getting accurate information. One major challenge, as psychology professor Lisa Fazio points out, is that most people do not take the time and effort to make sure that the "facts" they hear are true. Instead, people default to the assumption that what they hear is reliable. Fazio states,

> As a society we function on the assumption that the vast majority of information we encounter will be true. Thus, when we encounter a new piece of information, like a piece of gossip from a neighbor, a cool science fact on Reddit, or a post on social media, we often don't search through our entire knowledge base to ask whether the information fits with what we already know. Instead, we simply consider that it's "good enough."[25]

Fazio points out that it is easy for people, even highly intelligent ones, to absorb incorrect information. She gives the example of a Duke University study conducted in the early

2000s of a phenomenon that scholars term *knowledge neglect*. It consists of a person focusing on one piece of information while inadvertently skipping over a second piece in the same statement. In the study, college students answered three questions. One asked how many animals Moses took on the ark, another asked which museum Michelangelo's *Mona Lisa* hangs in, and the last asked which phrase follows Macbeth's "To be or not to be" soliloquy. Fazio writes,

> If you're like many readers, you may have answered the questions without noticing the errors within. It was of course Noah, not Moses, who took the animals on the ark; Leonardo da Vinci painted the Mona Lisa; and that soliloquy is from Hamlet, not Macbeth. Yet [the students in the Duke study] failed to notice the error in 41 percent of similarly distorted questions.[26]

People tend to assume that things they read are true, and they do not always carefully evaluate information they read on social media sites, such as Twitter.

Because the students recognized one piece of valid information—for example, "To be or not to be" is part of a Shakespearean soliloquy—they assumed the rest of each question was not intending to mislead them.

Trouble Separating Fact from Opinion

Fazio and other experts often use the knowledge neglect example to show how easy it is to be misled when taking in information. Such small errors, they explain, are only one aspect of a bigger problem in which people frequently have trouble distinguishing verified facts from opinions or false information. Moreover, the media experts at the University of Washington Libraries system say that the problem is amplified by a second difficulty: "not all information is created equal." Using the example of the internet, these experts point out that anyone "can publish on the Web. There is no editor, fact checker, or peer review process for the 'free' content that is available on [that platform]."[27]

The fact that many Americans, as well as people in other countries, often fail to separate facts from opinion or fiction was proved in a highly revealing 2018 Pew Research Center survey. Amy Mitchell and other Pew researchers sought to measure average Americans' ability to tell the difference between five factual statements and five opinion statements. The result was that most of the survey subjects correctly identified at least three of the five statements in each set.

> "Not all information is created equal."[27]
>
> —University of Washington Libraries

The problem, the researchers assert, is that getting three out of five questions right is only slightly better than if the subjects randomly guessed. Far fewer of them got all five questions right, and about a quarter got most or all the questions wrong. "Even more revealing," they state, "is that certain Americans do far better at parsing through this content than others. Those with high political awareness, those who are very digitally savvy, and those who place

A Difference of Opinion on Fact-Checkers

Most Americans think that the leading online fact-checking sites, including PolitiFact and Snopes, tend to be largely unbiased and reliable. Yet a minority of members of the two major US political parties sometimes claim the fact-checkers are not as impartial as they claim to be. Moreover, these critics are not evenly split by political affiliation. According to a 2019 Pew Research Center study, for reasons that are somewhat unclear, the complaints come far more often from the Republican side. In the words of the study's authors,

> Members of the two parties do not see eye-to-eye on this question. Seven-in-ten Republicans say fact-checkers tend to favor one side, compared with roughly three-in-ten Democrats (29%), a 41 percentage point difference. Conversely, most Democrats (69%) say fact-checkers deal fairly with all sides, a view shared by just 28% of Republicans. Independents are more split, with 47% saying fact-checkers tend to favor one side and 51% saying they deal fairly with all sides. [It should be noted that] independents who lean toward the Democratic Party and those who lean toward the Republican Party diverge sharply (65% vs. 37% saying fact-checkers deal fairly with all sides, respectively).

Mason Walker and Jeffrey Gottfried, "Republicans Far More Likely than Democrats to Say Fact-Checkers Tend to Favor One Side," Pew Research Center, June 27, 2019. www.pewresearch.org.

high levels of trust in the news media are better able than others to accurately identify news-related statements as factual or opinion."[28]

The same study also concluded that political party identification affects the way Americans try to separate facts from opinion or false information. "Both Republicans and Democrats show a propensity to be influenced by which side of the [political] aisle a statement appeals to most," the researchers explain. "For example, members of each political party were more likely to label both factual and opinion statements as factual when they appealed more to their political side."[29]

Are Social Media Platforms Reliable News Sources?

Despite these difficulties, Mitchell and other experts point out, almost anyone can learn to spot false information. A variety of books and online articles and videos provide tips to make people more savvy consumers of information.

The best tip is to carefully consider the source of the information to determine whether it is reliable or questionable. In many cases, the source of daily information is likely to be Facebook, Twitter, or some other social media platform because, as a 2021 Pew study found, 48 percent, or nearly half, of US adults get news from social media often or at least sometimes. Scholars who study information distribution and social trends find that statistic disturbing because study after study has found that social media sites are the dominant platforms that spread false information.

One reason for this frequent lack of factual accuracy, explain the researchers in the University of Washington Libraries system, is that "traditional authorship and publishing rules don't always apply in social media." In fact, they say, "anyone with a [computer or smartphone] can author and share (or publish) social media content." That means that individuals with little or no expertise in a specific field can still publish their personal opinions and pass them off as factual, or someone may interpret them in that manner. Thus, the researchers remark, social media content "may be fact, opinion, or fake." It may be written "by professional organizations who employ fact checkers *or* your high school friend who re-posts every conspiracy theory he reads about. . . . Anything goes in social media, so it's up to each of us to evaluate content and determine its reliability."[30]

People who rely almost exclusively on social media for their news are not only more likely to be misled, but they also are less well informed than those who use other, more reliable news sources. According to a Pew study published in July 2020,

Americans who rely primarily on social media for news . . . tend to know less about the 2020 election, less about the coronavirus pandemic, and less about political news in general than people who rely on news websites, cable or network TV, radio, and print. Those who depend on social media are also more likely than other news consumers to be exposed to made-up news, such as the conspiracy theory that powerful people planned the pandemic and invented the coronavirus in a lab, and to give credence to falsehoods.[31]

For these reasons, almost all impartial experts say that following Facebook and other social media is fine for sharing personal information and family news with relatives and friends. But users should avoid getting the news of the day from such sources.

Checking News Sources for Bias

According to the experts, the best news sources are print media (newspapers and magazines) and broadcast media (television and radio). Most print and broadcast sources have online outlets, which are convenient for obtaining brief overviews of the latest news stories.

Many people tend to choose print and broadcast news sources that seem to match their own political biases. And in some cases, certain sources freely and publicly admit that their content is designed to appeal to people who lean either left or right. It is widely accepted, for instance, that among mainstream television news networks, Fox News aims at a right-of-center audience and MSNBC leans toward a left-of-center audience.

Still, those two widely watched networks have many competitors, and each one has its own slant. Nonetheless, a few broadcast networks and other news sources aim more for the political middle to provide a more balanced view of events.

Seeing a need for an easier way to differentiate among the biases of the numerous news sources, in 2018 attorney Vanessa Otera created Ad Fontes Media. An impartial platform, it does not label information sources as either good or bad. Nor

"Those who depend on social media are also more likely than other news consumers to be exposed to made-up news."[31]

—Pew Research Center

does it recommend certain ones over others (except for a handful of obviously bogus programs that endorse nonsensical or dangerous conspiracy theories, such as Alex Jones's *Infowars*). Instead, Ad Fontes carefully analyzes sources for the way they lean politically on a consistent basis in article after article. Then it rates them according to their degree of both bias and factual accuracy. Those ratings form a colorful graph known as the Media Bias Chart. The news sources that lie roughly in the chart's middle, which tend not to lean very far toward either the right or left, include Reuters News Agency, the British Broadcasting Corporation (BBC), the Public Broadcasting Service (PBS), *USA Today*, the *Wall Street Journal*, the *New York Times*, and the *Washington Post*.

Fact-Checking for Accuracy

In addition to Ad Fontes and its convenient chart, questionable news items can be quickly debunked on reliable online fact-checking platforms. Among the best, say researchers with the

Young People Are Better at Separating Fact from Opinion

A 2018 survey by the Pew Research Center found that younger Americans are better than older ones at recognizing the difference between factual statements and mere opinion. The survey's authors reported that

> 63% of 18- to 49-year-olds correctly identified the following factual statement . . . "Spending on Social Security, Medicare, and Medicaid make up the largest portion of the U.S. federal budget." About half of those ages 50 and older (51%) correctly classified the same statement. Additionally, 18- to 49-year-olds were 12 percentage points more likely than those at least 50 years of age (60% vs. 48%, respectively) to correctly categorize the following factual statement . . . "Immigrants who are in the U.S. illegally have some rights under the Constitution." Among the opinion statements, roughly three-quarters of 18- to 49-year-olds (77%) correctly identified the following opinion statement . . . "Government is almost always wasteful and inefficient," compared with about two-thirds of older Americans (65%). And younger Americans were slightly more likely than older adults (82% vs. 78%, respectively) to correctly categorize this opinion statement . . . "Abortion should be legal in most cases."

Jeffrey Gottfried and Elizabeth Grieco, "Younger Americans Are Better than Older Americans at Telling Factual News Statements from Opinions," Pew Research Center, October 23, 2018. www.pewresearch.org.

Eastern Washington University Libraries, are FactCheck.org, PolitiFact, Snopes, and the *Washington Post* Fact Checker. The researchers point out that these platforms "have no overt political bias."[32] So, whatever they may say about a politician, speech, policy, or specific incident or claim can generally be trusted as unbiased.

People visit fact-checking platforms to test the accuracy of a controversial claim, and most sites convey their conclusions through easy-to-understand rating systems. For example, PolitiFact, created by the *Tampa Bay Times* in 2007, employs a system it lightheartedly calls its "Truth-o-Meter." A claim to be evaluated for accuracy will register on its scale as one of the following: "True," "Mostly True," "Half True," "Mostly False," "False," or, in the case of an outright lie, "Pants on Fire."

Similarly, the *Washington Post*'s rating system uses a scale of so-called Pinocchios (based on the fairy-tale character whose nose grew longer when he told a lie). On that scale, a somewhat misleading statement earns one Pinocchio, and four Pinocchios are awarded to an outright lie. Meanwhile, Snopes's rating scale includes "True," "Mostly True," "Mixture," "Mostly False," "False," "Unproven," and "Legend." Supposed facts that end up with a "Legend" rating are viewed to be so vague and unsubstantiated that they are considered impossible to either prove or disprove.

Look for Opposing Views and Recognize Emotional Manipulation

Some people prefer not to use ready-made tools, such as Ad Fontes and the various fact-checking sites, and instead examine various information sources on their own. That way, they hope, they will be able to judge for themselves which sources are best for them personally. One way to determine the reliability of a questionable statement or claim made in the news is to find corroborating evidence, says Texas-based photojournalist and information specialist John Bogna. "If something seems especially crazy," he says,

> look for additional coverage and read multiple sources. If the article you see has only one source, dig deeper on the publication. Chances are the story may not be true. Do a web search on the article's author. Read the publication's "about" page. Look up the website's publisher to see what their views are. You might find strong evidence of bias, either in the article itself, the site's info, or both.[33]

In addition to finding such backup evidence, Bogna explains, one can further clarify either the validity or meaning of the content or claim by seeking out opposing views. If the information sounds biased too much toward the political left, readers should check

out the same story on a somewhat right-leaning source such as the *Wall Street Journal*. Conversely, if the information appears to be biased toward the right, curious individuals can check to see if MSNBC has reported on it. Or they can seek more balanced coverage on the middle-of-the-road *PBS NewsHour* or NPR.

Still another method of determining the reliability of a news story is to consider the emotional state of the speaker or writer. If it appears that the author is upset, angry, or afraid—and is urging readers to feel the same way—the source probably intends to manipulate readers. "Look out for strong emotional triggers," Bogna warns:

> Does the content leave you feeling outraged? Terrified? Upset? Chances are it was engineered to do just that so that you'll share it and spread the message without even thinking. . . . Sharing a viral post spreads the message of that post like a sneeze spreads the flu. Research shows

emotional messages spread more widely within our networks because they get more engagement. . . . Angry messages get shared widely, but so do "feel-good" posts designed to play on impulses other than outrage. This is because the reasons people share bad information vary from outrage, to boosting their own self-image, to informing others. So we might share a story that seems warm and fuzzy because we . . . think it will make us look like better people to those in our network.[34]

However a person manages to separate facts from fiction and real news from fake news, today doing so is more crucial than ever, says Rosalind Tedford, an expert on how false information harms human societies. People need to think carefully about "the rise of mis/disinformation and the impact it has on our lives, our relationships, and our democracy," she says. "It is critical to understand why it's such an effective tool, how to behave when we encounter it, and how to avoid it as much as possible."[35]

"The reasons people share bad information vary from outrage, to boosting their own self-image, to informing others."[34]

—John Bogna, photojournalist and information specialist

CHAPTER FOUR

How Can Misinformation Be Counteracted?

After Donald Trump lost the 2020 presidential election to Joe Biden, Trump's legal team went to the courts. It brought cases before more than sixty judges across the country, insisting that the outcome should be overturned because of alleged widespread voter fraud. But these efforts were unsuccessful. One judge after another, including several whom Trump had appointed, rejected his claims.

This did not sit well with many of Trump's supporters, who had come to believe that the election had been stolen. And some of them loudly complained on social media and other information venues. One such grievance took the form of an Instagram post on October 25, 2022, which read, "It's not that there is no evidence the election was stolen, but that no court had the guts to hear the evidence. They dismissed the cases, not the evidence. They refused to look at it, because the price of getting involved was too high. This is how evil destroys a republic."[36]

Though apparently well-meaning, the author of the post was misinformed. PolitiFact and several other impartial fact-checking sites carefully looked into the way the court cases in question had transpired. They found that it was true that some judges tossed out Trump's lawsuits for procedural reasons. However, several of the judges did look at the "evidence" presented and concluded that there was no proof of any voter fraud on the level that would be needed to change the election results.

In Nevada, for instance, on December 2, 2020, district court judge James T. Russell dismissed the case Trump's lawyers had brought before him. In his decision, he stated that they had failed "to provide credible and relevant evidence" to contest the election results. They "did not prove under any standard of proof that illegal votes were cast and counted or legal votes were not counted at all, due to voter fraud."[37]

Many Americans were thankful that the nation's courts had overwhelmingly declared that the former president's claims of election fraud were bogus. It assured them that some of the nation's institutions were functioning in good faith. Meanwhile, some people also noted that such legal procedures and decisions could have a larger application beyond the results of any single case—namely, the courts could potentially be used to fight back against the flood of false information plaguing modern society.

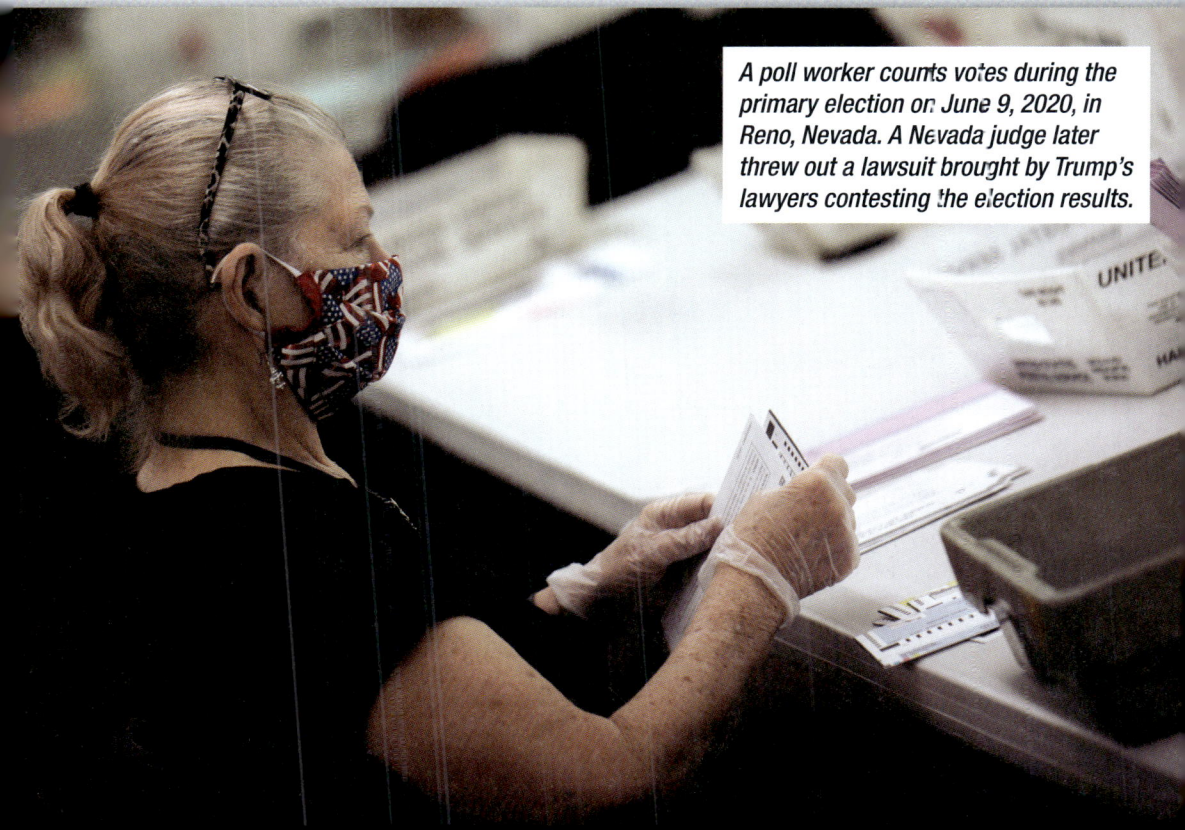

A poll worker counts votes during the primary election on June 9, 2020, in Reno, Nevada. A Nevada judge later threw out a lawsuit brought by Trump's lawyers contesting the election results.

Passing New Laws Against False Information

A 2019 Pew Research Center survey confirmed that most Americans think false news is a serious problem that needs to be counteracted or weeded out. The survey team found that

> more Americans view made-up news as a very big problem for the country than identify terrorism, illegal immigration, racism, and sexism that way. Additionally, nearly seven-in-ten U.S. adults (68%) say made-up news and information greatly impacts Americans' confidence in government institutions, and roughly half (54%) say it is having a major impact on our confidence in each other.[38]

Still, Americans are unsure about how to reduce the spread of misinformation and fake news. Going to court and having judges or juries try to separate fact from fiction does work in individual cases, but launching litigation every time a fake news story arises seems impractical.

Several other solutions have been proposed, however. One of the more promising may also be one of the more difficult to implement. It consists of creating new legislation, especially on the federal level, to regulate information and punish those who trade in disinformation. "We currently have a legislative framework that limits the ability of certain industries—tobacco and pharmaceuticals—to advertise their products and to spread misinformation," say professors Cailan O'Connor and James O. Weatherall.

> "More Americans view made-up news as a very big problem for the country than identify terrorism, illegal immigration, racism, and sexism that way."[38]
>
> —Pew Research Center

> This is because there is a clear public health risk to allowing these industries to promote their products. . . . We think these legislative frameworks should be extended to cover more general efforts to spread misinformation. In an

era of global warming, websites like Breitbart News and Infowars are more damaging to public health than Joe Camel and the Marlboro Man were in the past, and they should be treated as such.[39]

This approach is already used in varying degrees in some European countries, especially Germany. There, laws enacted between 2016 and 2020, prohibit social media companies from letting false, harmful content remain posted on their sites. Some people see this as censorship that would violate US constitutional protections of free speech. However, O'Connor and Weatherall remark that "the goal here is not to limit speech. It is to prevent speech from illegitimately posing as something it is not, and to prevent [the spread of] damaging propaganda."[40] In any case, the worry that new anti–fake news laws might encourage undue censorship is one of the foremost factors preventing the passage of such legislation in the United States.

A Professional Journalist's Favorite Information Sources

Paul Glader, a distinguished professor of journalism at The King's College in New York City, says he is highly concerned that students as well as other members of society do not always find and utilize more accurate, reliable sources of news and information. "In the post-truth age," he says,

that is, an age when one has to work hard to be media literate and find the truthful sources of information, citizens should support local and regional publications that [stick] to ethical journalism standards. . . . Realizing that millions [of] people are scratching their heads wondering what to read and where to spend their subscription dollars, here are my top 10 large journalistic brands, where I believe you can most often find real, reported facts.

Glader goes on to list the *Wall Street Journal*, the *New York Times*, the BBC, the *Washington Post*, the *New Yorker*, *The Economist*, the big three wire services (the Associated Press, Reuters, and Bloomberg News), *Foreign Affairs*, *The Atlantic*, and Politico.

Paul Glader, "Journalism Brands Where You Can Find Real Facts Rather than Alternative Facts," in H.W. Wilson, *Propaganda and Misinformation*. Amenia, NY: Grey House, 2020, pp. 153–55.

Networks of Teens and Other Volunteers

While Germany and a few other European countries were passing laws to rein in false information, the European Union (an alliance of most European nations) also tackled the problem because of disinformation surrounding the COVID-19 pandemic. That organization initiated a program tasked with identifying and combating fake news. In part, it utilizes an antidisinformation tool consisting of a network of citizen-volunteers from various nations. Their job is to look for and then debunk false information and work with social media platforms to eliminate it. Although some of these volunteers are adults, many are teenagers who are highly adept at using computers, smartphones, and other electronic communications equipment.

Some media experts have advocated for the formation of such a network of teens and older volunteers in the United States. If em-

On Tuesday, March 14, 2023, students work together at MisinfoDay, an event hosted by the University of Washington in Seattle to help high schoolers identify and avoid misinformation.

powered, they would operate as watchdogs who would fact-check stories and claims on the internet, including social media. They would then correct any false information they find and publish the true facts.

Proponents believe that, over time, the teens and twenty-somethings involved in such a program would pass on what they learn to friends and fellow students. In that way, the initial volunteers would become the foundation for a widespread educational movement among young people about the pitfalls of misinformation. And, eventually, such skills likely would be taught as a matter of course in middle schools and high schools. As Joanne Orlando, a digital media specialist, points out, "With the right tools, [young people] can assess credible information for themselves." Through proper education and training, therefore, they can develop "their understanding of the online world." Orlando says this is about empowering "children to understand and assess the usefulness of information for themselves."[41] Building media literacy is part of the European Union's effort, and many Americans believe it should be strengthened in US education.

New Jersey took a big step in this direction in January 2023, when the governor signed into law a bill that requires the teaching of media literacy in kindergarten through twelfth grade. The aim of the new law is to teach students to think critically about the information they read or hear—especially online—where it comes from, whether it contains facts or opinions, and more. According to Republican state senator Mike Testa, teaching children to be media literate will help them to separate news from opinion in social media and online.

New Jersey governor Phil Murphy noted that America's democracy is struggling under an assault of disinformation that often erodes the truth and trust in the institutions on which democracy depends. The governor added that requiring young people to learn the difference between fact and fiction—and to better understand information in all its forms—will help fight this erosion.

Four Moves That Make Teens Better Fact-Checkers

University of Washington scholar Mike Caulfield gives the following helpful advice to teens who choose to fact-check news and information sources on their own:

> What people need most when confronted with a claim that may not be 100% true [are] *things they can do to get closer to the truth*. They need something I have decided to call "moves.". . .
>
> - Check for previous work: Look around to see if someone else has already fact-checked the claim. . . .
> - Go "upstream" to the source of the claim. Most web content is not original. . . .
> - Read laterally: Once you get to the source of a claim, read what other people say about the source (publication, author, etc.). The truth is in the network.
> - Circle back: If you get lost [or] hit dead ends . . . back up and start over knowing what you know now. You're likely to take a more informed path with different search terms and better decisions. . . .
>
> When you encounter a claim you want to check, your first move might be to see if sites like *Politifact* or *Snopes* . . . have researched the claim.

Mike Caulfield, "Web Literacy for Student Fact-Checkers: Four Moves," Pressbooks, January 8, 2017. https://pressbooks.pub.

New Algorithms to Fight False Information

Passing new state and national laws against spreading fake news and equipping armies of watchdogs to police the internet and broadcast news are massive, complicated approaches to fighting false information. In part, this is why some experts advocate employing some less complex and labor-intensive methods. One approach that has been increasingly talked about in recent years is creating automated systems that will detect and hopefully correct false information on the internet.

Such a system would utilize precisely designed computer algorithms, or a set of instructions programmed to solve a given problem or perform a specific computation. For example, a computer algorithm can be used to detect certain words, phrases, patterns, and so forth that appear on the internet. In their 2019 book about misinformation, O'Connor and Weatherall propose that specialized algorithms should be used "to identify fake news and *prevent* it from being amplified on [specific online] sites, or even prevent fake news from being shared on such sites at all."[42]

Rudimentary versions of such algorithms have already been used by technicians at Facebook to let users know that a certain sentence or paragraph contains a statement that might not be true. But these algorithms are not designed to detect false information that appears on multiple platforms and in multiple languages. Media experts point out that something on that scale requires more sophisticated algorithms.

Rising to that challenge, in 2021 computer scientists from MIT, the University of Michigan, and Oxford University teamed up to begin developing a highly effective antimisinformation algorithm. As Scott A. Hale, an Oxford University professor and researcher, explains,

> The algorithm is the first of its kind to be able to group social media messages making similar fact-checkable claims across a range of languages. By doing so, the algorithm can help fact-checkers reach a wider audience and help users understand if the message they have received via their messaging app has been fact-checked. For example, the algorithm can find [multiple] messages with similar claims.[43]

According to Hale, this new type of algorithm does more than simply search through an online text to find specific words; it also knows how to recognize the meaning of, or an idea voiced within, phrases, sentences, and groups of sentences. Plus, it can detect a true or false meaning or idea even when it is expressed using a different set of words. In addition, it can do all this in several different languages. Looking at the future use of such algorithms to combat fake news, Hale says, "It is very rewarding to develop new approaches that can empower fact-checkers and ensure their work is more discoverable."[44]

Are Falsehoods Inevitable on Social Media?

Many media and technology experts feel that the ongoing development of such sophisticated algorithms holds great promise for reducing the amount of false information constantly spreading through society. The key problem, they say, is that such advanced technology is not being applied quickly and widely enough. As late as 2023, social media sites—by far the largest platforms for fake news—were not yet using algorithms capable of detecting and blocking most false information.

A study published in the *Proceedings of the National Academy of Sciences* in January 2023 determined the leading reason for this troubling policy. Conducted by researchers at the University of Southern California (USC), the study surveyed 2,476 active Facebook users ranging in age from eighteen to eighty-nine. "Our finding," says USC professor of psychology Wendy Wood, is that misinformation is primarily "a function of the structure of the social media sites themselves."[45]

More specifically, the study shows that the chief algorithms used by Facebook and other social media companies are not designed to filter out false content; instead, their main function is to make sure that users remain on a site and share information for as long as possible. Due to that approach, Wood explains, "users form habits of sharing information that gets recognition from others. Once habits form, information sharing is automatically activated by cues on the platform without users considering critical response outcomes, such as spreading misinformation."[46]

> "It is very rewarding to develop new approaches that can empower fact-checkers and ensure their work is more discoverable."[44]
>
> —Scott A. Hale, professor at the Oxford Internet Institute, Oxford University

Social media sites are not designed to filter out misinformation. Their purpose is to boost popular content, which can lead to the spread of sensational but false stories.

Thus, many users remain on the site for longer periods than they would have if not manipulated by the site's operators. And while on the site, those users frequently share information with fellow users. Moreover, because some of that data consists of false information, the longer they stay on the site, the more falsehoods they tend to spread. The study's authors were surprised to find that, on average, the survey's participants spread two and even three times as many falsehoods as the few users who stayed on the site only briefly. Even worse, the users who stayed on the site the longest spread six times more fake news than the ones who stayed for only a short time.

Perhaps the study's most important finding of all was that such sites do not have to operate this way. Near the end of the survey, the researchers intervened and promised small rewards for those users who shared only information they were certain was true. The result was that the amount of accurate information shared doubled. Therefore, says communications specialist Pamela Madrid, social media users can "be incentivized to [become] more sensitive to sharing truthful content."[47] And that means that fake news is not an inevitable part of social media content.

The Ultimate Responsibility

Besides demonstrating that social media platforms need to do more to slow the spread of false information, the USC study revealed an important fact about consumers of news and information—namely, that many ordinary people tend to inadvertently spread misinformation online. So, they, like the those who distribute news via the internet, print, or broadcast news, bear some of the blame for the proliferation of fake facts.

Indeed, says psychology professor Lisa Fazio, the ultimate responsibility for slowing and hopefully someday stopping the flow of false information lies with us—the ordinary members of society. New laws, fact-checkers, and advanced algorithms can all help fight fake news. But in the final analysis, those who purposely propagate it will fail if most people refuse to believe and accept it. As Fazio argues,

> While the problem of misinformation can seem overwhelming, it's important to remember that all of us as individuals can play a role in improving the quality of information we see. We control what spreads on social media and can be responsible for what we share and publicize. We all have a responsibility to promote accurate information online. Don't share stories without reading them first, and double-check information when it feels too good to be true. But mostly, take a breath and pause. Rely on your brain, not your gut.[48]

SOURCE NOTES

Introduction: Two Kinds of False Information

1. Marcel Bruins, "How to Define Fake News, Misinformation, and Disinformation." European Seed, September 8, 2022. https://european-seed.com.
2. Quoted in Laura A. Bischoff, "GOP-Invited Ohio Doctor Sherri Tenpenny Falsely Tells Ohio Lawmakers COVID-19 Shots 'Magnetize' People, Create 5G 'Interfaces.'" *Columbus (OH) Dispatch*, June 23, 2021. www.dispatch.com.
3. Quoted in Bischoff, "GOP-Invited Ohio Doctor Sherri Tenpenny Falsely Tells Ohio Lawmakers COVID-19 Shots 'Magnetize' People, Create 5G 'Interfaces.'"
4. Natalie Marchant, "Omicron Has Seen a Surge in COVID Misinformation. 2 Experts Explain How to Combat It," World Economic Forum, January 31, 2022. www.weforum.org.

Chapter One: Causes and Spread of False Information

5. Cailin O'Connor and James O. Weatherall, "How Misinformation Spreads and Why We Trust It," *Scientific American*, September 1, 2019. www.scientificamerican.com.
6. Chris Meserole, "How Misinformation Spreads on Social Media—and What to Do About It," *Order from Chaos* (blog), Brookings Institution, May 9, 2018. www.brookings.edu.
7. Quoted in Kim Mills, "Episode 124: Why People Believe in Conspiracy Theories, with Karen Douglas, PhD," *Speaking of Psychology* (podcast), American Psychological Association, January 10, 2021. www.apa.org.
8. Quoted in Mills, "Episode 124."
9. Nicholas A. Ashford, "Not on Facebook? You're Still Likely Being Fed Misinformation," *New York Times*, March 29, 2021. www.nytimes.com.
10. Ashford, "Not on Facebook?"
11. Ian Klein, "Enemy of the People: The Ghost of the F.C.C. Fairness Doctrine in the Age of Alternative Facts," *Hastings Communications and Entertainment Law Journal*, vol. 42, no. 1, 2020. https://repository.uchastings.edu.
12. Klein, "Enemy of the People."

13. Lisa Fazio, "Fact or Fake? The Role of Knowledge Neglect in Misinformation," Vanderbilt University, May 15, 2020. https://news.vanderbilt.edu.
14. Quoted in Jonathan Weisman, "For Trump's G.O.P., Crossing Lines Has Few Consequences," *New York Times*, April 23, 2022. www.nytimes.com.
15. Cailan O'Connor and James O. Weatherall, *The Misinformation Age: How False Beliefs Spread*. New Haven, CT: Yale University Press, 2019, pp. 11–12.

Chapter Two: How False Information Is Damaging Society

16. Cecilia Kang and Sheera Frenkel, "'PizzaGate' Conspiracy Theory Thrives Anew in the TikTok Era," *New York Times*, June 27, 2020. www.nytimes.com.
17. Sarah McCammon and Liz Baker, "Disinformation Fuels Distrust and Even Violence at All Levels of Government," National Public Radio, March 1, 2021. www.npr.org.
18. Gabriel R. Sanchez, Keesha Middlemass, and Aila Rodriguez, "Misinformation Is Eroding the Public's Confidence in Democracy," *FixGov* (blog), Brookings Institution, July 26, 2022. www.brookings.edu.
19. Hannah Hartig, "In Their Own Words: How Americans Reacted to the Rioting at the U.S. Capitol," Pew Research Center, January 15, 2021. www.pewresearch.org.
20. Lee Rainie, "Trust in America: Do Americans Trust the News Media?," Pew Research Center, January 5, 2022. www.pewresearch.org.
21. David A. Graham, "Some Real News About Fake News," *The Atlantic*, June 7, 2019. www.theatlantic.com.
22. Center for Information Technology and Society, "The Danger of Fake News in Inflaming or Suppressing Social Conflict." www.cits.ucsb.edu.
23. Jonathan Corpus Ong, "Online Disinformation Against AAPI Communities During the COVID-19 Pandemic," Carnegie Endowment for International Peace, October 19, 2021. https://carnegieendowment.org.
24. Sebastiaan van der Lans, "Buzzword or Real Threat? Fake News Is More Dangerous than You Think," *Forbes*, March 26, 2021. www.forbes.com.

Chapter Three: Distinguishing Facts from Misinformation

25. Fazio, "Fact or Fake?"
26. Fazio, "Fact or Fake?"
27. University of Washington Libraries, "Savvy Info Consumers: Evaluating Information," August 17, 2022. https://guides.lib.uw.edu.
28. Amy Mitchell et al., "Distinguishing Between Factual and Opinion Statements in the News," Pew Research Center, June 18, 2018. www.pewresearch.org.
29. Mitchell et al., "Distinguishing Between Factual and Opinion Statements in the News."
30. University of Washington Libraries, "Savvy Info Consumers: Social Media." August 17, 2022. https://guides.lib.uw.edu.

31. Tom Infield, "Americans Who Get News Mainly on Social Media Are Less Knowledgeable and Less Engaged," *Trust*, November 16, 2020. www.pew trusts.org

32. Eastern Washington University Libraries, "Fact-Checking Sites," November 2, 2022. https://research.ewu.edu.

33. John Bogna, "Be Careful What You Post: How to Tell the Difference Between Fact and Fake News," *PC Magazine*, October 26, 2022. www.pc mag.com.

34. Bogna, "Be Careful What You Post."

35. Quoted in Cheryl Walker, "Facts and Fake News: How to Tell the Difference," Wake Forest News, January 20, 2021. https://news.wfu.edu.

Chapter Four: How Can Misinformation Be Counteracted?

36. Quoted in Madison Czopek, "Courts Did Review Trump Campaign 'Evidence' of Election Fraud. Claims That Say Otherwise Are Wrong," Politi-Fact, October 28, 2022. www.politifact.com.

37. Quoted in Czopek, "Courts Did Review Trump Campaign 'Evidence' of Election Fraud."

38. Amy Mitchell et al., "Many Americans Say Made-Up News Is a Critical Problem That Needs to Be Fixed," Pew Research Center, June 5, 2019. www.pewresearch.org.

39. O'Connor and Weatherall, *The Misinformation Age*, pp. 182–83.

40. O'Connor and Weatherall, *The Misinformation Age*, p. 183.

41. Joanne Orlando, "How to Help Kids Navigate Fake News and Misinformation Online," in H.W. Wilson, *Reference Shelf: Propaganda and Misinformation*. Amenia, NY: Grey House, 2020, p. 146.

42. O'Connor and Weatherall, *The Misinformation Age*, p. 174.

43. Scott A. Hale, "Tackling Misinformation One Algorithm at a Time," Oxford Internet Institute, June 9, 2021. www.oii.ox.ac.uk.

44. Hale, "Tackling Misinformation One Algorithm at a Time."

45. Quoted in Pamela Madrid, "USC Study Reveals the Key Reason Why Fake News Spreads on Social Media," USC News, January 17, 2023. https://news.usc.edu.

46. Quoted in Madrid, "USC Study Reveals the Key Reason Why Fake News Spreads on Social Media."

47. Madrid, "USC Study Reveals the Key Reason Why Fake News Spreads on Social Media."

48. Fazio, "Fact or Fake?"

Books

Ben Boyington et al., *The Media and Me: A Guide to Critical Media Literacy for Young People*. New York: Triangle Square, 2022.

Kathryn Hulick, *Media Literacy: Information and Disinformation*. San Diego, CA: ReferencePoint, 2023.

Hal Marcovitz, *Media Bias: What Is It and Why Does It Matter?* San Diego, CA: ReferencePoint, 2023.

Barbara Sheen, *The Fake News Crisis: How Misinformation Harms Society*. San Diego, CA: ReferencePoint, 2022.

Chris Sperry and Cyndy Scheibe, *Teaching Students to Decode the World: Media Literacy and Critical Thinking Across the Curriculum*. London: Association for Supervision and Curriculum Development, 2022.

Seema Yasmin, *What the Fact? Finding the Truth in All the Noise*. New York: Simon & Schuster, 2022.

Internet Sources

Jessica Brandt and Valerie Wirtschafter, "How Russia Spreads Propaganda About Ukraine in Latin America and the Impact of Platform Responses," Brookings Institution, December 2022. www.brookings.edu.

Council of Europe, "Dealing with Propaganda, Misinformation, and Fake News." ww.coe.int.

Drew DeSilver, "Q&A: Telling the Difference Between Factual and Opinion Statements in the News," Pew Research Center, June 18, 2018. www.pewresearch.org.

Erika Edwards, "Vaccine Misinformation One of the Biggest Public Health Threats, CDC Director Says," NBC News, December 16, 2022. www.nbcnews.com.

Daniel Funke and Daniele Flamini, "A Guide to Anti-misinformation Actions Around the World," Poynter Institute, February 20, 2023. www.poynter.org.

Christian Jarrett, "A Psychologist Explains Why People Believe in Conspiracy Theories," *BBC Science Focus*, January 5, 2022. www.sciencefocus.com.

Mark Lynas, "COVID: Top 10 Current Conspiracy Theories," *Alliance for Science* (blog), April 20, 2020. https://allianceforscience.cornell.edu.

Greg Miller, "Researchers Are Tracking Another Pandemic, Too—of Coronavirus Misinformation," *Science*, March 24, 2020. www.science.org.

Kim Mills, "Episode 124: Why People Believe in Conspiracy Theories, with Karen Douglas, PhD," *Speaking of Psychology* (podcast), American Psychological Association, January 10, 2021. ww.apa.org.

Cailin O'Connor and James O. Weatherall, "How Misinformation Spreads and Why We Trust It," *Scientific American*, September 1, 2019. www.scientific american.com.

Penn State University Libraries, "Evaluating Information." https://libraries.psu.edu.

Organizations and Websites

FactCheck.org
www.factcheck.org
FactCheck.org is a nonpartisan, nonprofit organization that advocates for the American public good by reducing the amount of deception and confusion in American politics and news reporting. The group carefully fact-checks political debates and speeches, television ads, and claims made in national news reporting.

News Literacy Project
https://newslit.org/for-everyone
The News Literacy Project tries to fight the ongoing flood of disinformation by giving people plenty of free online resources. These include a regular podcast, tips on how to identify fake information, and quizzes and other activities designed to sharpen readers' literary skills.

Pew Research Center
www.pewresearch.org/topic/news-habits-media/media-society/misinformation
The Pew Research Center's website includes a "Misinformation" section with a large collection of articles covering diverse topics related to information technology and how it can be twisted or perverted. One article, for example, is titled "More Americans Now Say Government Should Take Steps to Restrict False Information Online than in 2018."

PolitiFact
www.politifact.com
Launched in 2007, PolitiFact is dedicated to fact-checking journalists and other investigators and presenters of news in order to support America's democracy. The group's mission is to look at both sides of each political issue and expose any purposeful distortions or mistakes in content.

Snopes
www.snopes.com
Owned by the Snopes Media Group, Snopes is the oldest and biggest of the various online fact-checking sites. Journalists, folklorists, and everyday readers use it as a valuable research tool to separate fact from misinformation in a nonpartisan, unbiased manner.

INDEX

PICTURE CREDITS

ABOUT THE AUTHOR

In addition to his numerous acclaimed volumes on ancient civilizations, historian Don Nardo has published several studies of modern medical, scientific, and educational topics and phenomena, including *Nanotechnology and Medicine, Careers in Education, Teen Guide to Mental Health, Science and Sustainable Energy*, and award-winning books on astronomy and space exploration. Nardo also composes and arranges orchestral music. He lives with his wife, Christine, in Massachusetts.